The Little Jeep Who Couldn't Beep

Bless THIS mess

Rosie J Williams

ILLUSTRATED BY CYNTHIA L WILLIAMS

The Little Jeep Who Couldn't Beep

Illustrated by Cynthia L. Williams

ISBN: Paperback: 978-1-64746-086-0
Hardback: 978-1-64746-087-7
E-book: 978-1-64746-088-4

Library of Congress Control Number: 2019920768

Published by Author Academy Elite
An imprint of Igniting Souls
PO Box 43
Powell, OH 43065

Printed and bound by Hall Commercial Printing and Ingram Spark

Page layout by Jetlaunch.com
Book cover by Debbie O'Byrne at Jetlaunch.com

ACKNOWLEDGMENTS

To my friend Adam Florence for donating an Army Jeep to restore and use in Point Man Ministries, to my talented daughters-in-law, illustrator Cyndi and editor Becky, to my son Dan for his excellent suggestions, and to my husband Steve, for never giving up on restoring "Marty Mutt."

This book is dedicated to my hand-picked beta readers:

Andi, Wyatt, Ben, Arthur, Wrigley and Graham, all seated on the curb in the fourth of July parade scene!

The Little Jeep
Who Couldn't Beep

Rosie J. Williams

ILLUSTRATED BY CYNTHIA L. WILLIAMS

AUTHOR ACADEMY elite

There once was an Army truck
Named Marty Mutt the Jeep.
His engine went vroom, vroom,
And his horn went Beep Beep Beep.

Honk! Honk! Honk!
Down the road he came
Carrying the soldiers
Over bumpy terrain.

After working so hard
The months turned to years.
His frame was all twisted
He'd stripped out his gears!

His windshield was broken,
And so was his horn.
His tires were flat,
His seat cover torn.

The rain came down
And washed off his dust.
But sadly ole' Marty
Had started to rust.

He didn't have a place
To lay his tired head.
So, Marty got moved
To the junkyard shed.

He couldn't beep his horn
Or see from his mirrors.
Marty was sad
But couldn't wipe his tears.

Creeeek, Creeeek, Creeeek
Went the old shed door,
And a kind man said
"Just what I'm looking for!"

The man was Sergeant Willie,
Who loved red, white and blue.
He wanted to make Marty Mutt
Just like new!

Then Sergeant Willie took him home
And patted Marty's hood.
He towed him to a special spot,
And Marty felt so good!

Sergeant Willie's workshop
Was crammed from head to toe,
'Cause he would pick up
tools and junk
Everywhere he'd go!

The hours of work were steady
Though it seemed to take forever.
Sergeant Willie worked so hard
Putting Marty back together.

He didn't give up.
There was pounding and grinding.
He put on his goggles
And sparks went a flying.

He installed a new windshield
And put on new tires.
He replaced the cushions
And rearranged the wires.

Sergeant Willie told Marty
"You're fixed and re-stored!"
He turned on the key,
And the new engine roared.

Willie's eyes gleamed
As he drove the little jeep
To a place of celebration,
Throwing candy from his seat!

Marty Mutt was good as new
And people lined the streets.
The engine went vroom, vroom,
And the horn went "Beep, Beep, Beep."

Bedtime Prayer

As I lay my head down and go to sleep
And think about the Little jeep
Like Sgt. Willie helped Marty to beep
I give you Lord, my heart to keep

You are gentle and kind, I know that You care
You are right and true and always fair
Thanks for your love and hearing my prayer
And for always, always being there

AMEN

By Rosie J. Williams
www.rosiejwilliams.com

16828408R00026